MR. BOUNCE

by Roger Hargreaves

Alastair,

I found this book and I
thought of you!
"Happy Birthday!"
loads â luv,
Rachel.
xxx

WORLD INTERNATIONAL

Mr Bounce was very small and like a rubber ball.

He just couldn't keep himself on the ground!

He bounced all over the place!

And, as you can imagine, that made things rather difficult.

SPECIAL OFFERS FOR MR MEN AND LITTLE MISS READERS

13/6
20p

In every Mr Men and Little Miss book you will find a special token.
Collect only six tokens and we will send you a super poster of your choice
featuring all your favourite Mr Men or Little Miss friends.

And for the first 4,000 readers we hear from, we will send you a
Mr Men activity pad* and a bookmark* as well – absolutely free!

Return this page with six tokens from Mr Men and/or Little Miss books to:
Marketing Department, World International Limited, Deanway Technology Centre,
Wilmslow Road, Handforth, Cheshire SK9 3FB.

Your name:_____

Address:_____

_____ Postcode: _____

Signature of parent or guardian: _____

I enclose **six** tokens – please send me a Mr Men poster ☐
I enclose **six** tokens – please send me a Little Miss poster ☐

We may occasionally wish to advise you of other children's books that
we publish. If you would rather we didn't, please tick this box ☐

*while stocks last   (Please note: this offer is limited to a maximum of two posters per household.)

Collect six of these tokens.
You will find one inside every
Mr Men and Little Miss book
which has this special offer.

1 TOKEN

Please remove this page carefully

Join the

MR.MEN & *little miss*

Club

Treat your child to membership of the long-awaited Mr Men & Little Miss Club and see their delight when they receive a personal letter from Mr Happy and Little Miss Giggles, a club badge **with their name on**, and a superb Welcome Pack. And imagine how thrilled they'll be to receive a card from the Mr Men and Little Misses on their birthday and at Christmas!

Take a look at all of the great things in the Welcome Pack, every one of them of superb quality (*see box right*). If it were

on sale in the shops, the Pack alone would cost around £12.00. But a year's membership, including all of the other Club benefits, costs just **£7.99** (plus 70p postage) with a 14 day money-back guarantee if you're not delighted.

To enrol your child please send **your** name, address and telephone number together with **your child's** full name, date of birth and address (including postcode) and a cheque or postal order for £8.69 (payable to Mr Men & Little Miss Club) to: Mr Happy, Happyland (Dept. WI), PO Box 142, Horsham RH13 5FJ. Or call 01403 242727 to pay by credit card.

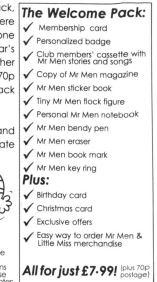

Please note: We reserve the right to change the terms of this offer (including the contents of the Welcome Pack) at any time but we offer a 14 day no-quibble money-back guarantee. We do not sell directly to children - all communications (except the Welcome Pack) will be via parents/guardians. After 31/12/96 please call to check that the price is still valid. Please allow 28 days for delivery. Promoter: Robell Media Promotions Limited, registered in England number 2852153.

The Welcome Pack:

✓ Membership card

✓ Personalized badge

✓ Club members' cassette with Mr Men stories and songs

✓ Copy of Mr Men magazine

✓ Mr Men sticker book

✓ Tiny Mr Men flock figure

✓ Personal Mr Men notebook

✓ Mr Men bendy pen

✓ Mr Men eraser

✓ Mr Men book mark

✓ Mr Men key ring

Plus:

✓ Birthday card

✓ Christmas card

✓ Exclusive offers

✓ Easy way to order Mr Men & Little Miss merchandise

All for just £7.99! (plus 70p postage)

Last week, for instance, Mr Bounce was out walking when he came to a farm.

He climbed over the farm gate, and you can guess what happened next, can't you?

He jumped down from the gate, and . . .

. . . bounced right into the duckpond!

BOUNCE went Mr Bounce.

SPLASH went Mr Bounce.

"QUACK," went the ducks.

The other morning, for instance, Mr Bounce was in bed.

He woke up, and jumped out of bed, and you can guess what happened next, can't you?

He bounced right out of his bedroom door and all the way downstairs.

Bouncebouncebouncebounce!

That happens quite often, which probably explains why Mr Bounce leaves his bedroom door open every night!

After he had picked himself up Mr Bounce went inside his house and sat down to think.

BOUNCE.

Mr Bounce bounced off the chair and banged his head on the ceiling.

BANG went Mr Bounce's head on the ceiling.

"OUCH!" said Mr Bounce.

"This is ridiculous," Mr Bounce thought to himself, rubbing his head. "I must do something to stop all this bouncing about."

He thought and thought.

"I know," he thought. "I'll go and see the doctor!"

So, after breakfast, Mr Bounce set off to the nearest town to see the doctor.

He was passing a tennis court when he tripped over a pebble.

BOUNCE he bounced.

And he bounced right on to the court where two children were playing tennis, and you can guess what happened next, can't you?

The children didn't realise that Mr Bounce wasn't a tennis ball, and started hitting him with their tennis racquets backwards and forwards over the net.

BOUNCE!

"OOO!"

BOUNCE!

"OW!"

BOUNCE!

"OUCH!"

Poor Mr Bounce.

Eventually, one of the children hit Mr Bounce so hard he bounced right out of the tennis court.

Mr Bounce bounced off down the road towards the town.

"Oh dear," he said, feeling very sorry for himself. "I've been bounced black and blue!"

A bus was coming down the road, and Mr Bounce decided that the safest place for him to be would be to be on it.

He got on and sat down, still feeling more than a little sorry for himself.

The bus drove into town.

The bus stopped right outside the doctor's.

Mr Bounce stepped down from the bus.

And you can guess what happened next, can't you?

He didn't step down on to the pavement outside the doctor's. Oh no, not Mr Bounce!

He stepped off the bus, and on to the pavement, and bounced, in through the doctor's window!

Dr Makeyouwell was sitting at his desk, enjoying his mid-morning cup of coffee.

Mr Bounce sailed through the open window, and landed . . .

Well, you can guess where he landed, can't you?

That's right!

SPLASH went the coffee.

"OUCH!" squeaked Mr Bounce. The coffee was rather hot.

"Good heavens," exclaimed Dr Makeyouwell.

After the doctor had fished Mr Bounce out of his coffee, and sat him on some blotting paper to dry out, he listened to what Mr Bounce had to tell him.

"So you see," said Mr Bounce finally, "you must give me something to stop me bouncing about all over the place quite so much."

"Hmmm," pondered the doctor.

After some thought Dr Makeyouwell went to his medicine cabinet and took out a pair of tiny red boots.

"This should do the trick," he told Mr Bounce. "Heavy boots! That should stop the bouncing!"

"Oh, thank you, Dr Makeyouwell," said Mr Bounce and walked home wearing his red boots.

Not bounced!

Walked!

That night Mr Bounce went to bed wearing his heavy boots.

And then he went to sleep.

The following morning, he woke up and yawned and stretched, and bounced out of bed.

And can you guess what happened next?

No, he didn't bounce down the stairs.

He went straight through the bedroom floorboards,

and finished up in the kitchen!